Levite Genes

A PRAISE AND WORSHIP MUSICAL FOR CHILDREN BY

Tracks Produced and Arranged by Chris Marion

Engraving and Piano Transcriptions by Allen Tuten, Compute-A-Chart

Performance Time: 45 minutes

COMPANION PRODUCTS:

Listening Cassette 0-7673-9007-5

Accompaniment Cassette 0-7673-9013-X
(Side A Split-track; Side B Instruments only)

Accompaniment CD 0-7673-9027-X
(Split-track and Stereo Tracks)

The Dovetailor 0-7673-9050-4
(Contains Teaching Materials, Activites, Posters, etc.)

Instructional/Movement Video 0-7673-9090-3

Promo Pak 0-7673-9052-0

A division of Genevox

0-7673-9008-3

A Word from the Author

Levite Genes is an easy to perform musical that leads children to an understanding of the privilege of leading in worship and praise. On this particular Sunday, choir directors Mr. Key and Mrs. Duffy extend an offer of free "Levite genes." The children quickly find that these "genes" can't be worn but, instead, represent an internal desire to worship the Lord – the new song God puts in our hearts.

Mrs. Duffy and Mr. Key take the children through a description of the Levites as the first worship leaders, then help them understand that having "Levite genes" is not dependent upon your birth, as it was for the Levites, but on a new birth in Jesus Christ.

Mrs. Starr, the ultimate stage mother, offers a humorous touch as she learns that her child doesn't need to have a solo or special part to lead worship, while Mrs. Duffy and Mr. Key help all the children understand that worship leads to service in many different expressions: singing, playing instruments, making costumes, and more.

In the end, everyone realizes there is preparation for worship, with the most important step being to ask Jesus into our hearts. Only then will we have *Levite Genes* in our soul.

Kathie Hill is the creator of *The Christmas Family Tree; Holly Day's Songs of Praise; Nic at Night; AmeriKids; Christmas in Egypt; Go, Go, Jonah;* and *The Don't Be Afraid Brigade,* all available through GENEVOX MUSIC GROUP.

Sequence

Setting

The close of a present day worship or chapel service.

Characters

Minister - your Pastor, Minister of Music, or Worship Leader (adult)
Mrs. Duffy - Children's Choir Director (adult)
Mr. Key - Children's Choir Director (adult)
Ruler - Mr. Key or a boy (*see Production Notes for options for "A
     Doorman for the Lord"*)
Boy - a boy (or girl, dressed as a boy)
Mrs. Starr - a stage mother (adult)
Lucy - Mrs. Starr's daughter (child)

*(Adult parts may be played by children, especially Mrs. Starr. Actors' real
names may be substituted for Minister, Mr. Key, and Mrs. Duffy, and the
latter may use their music stands to keep a copy of the script and score to
help with their many lines.)*

Choir Members

There are sixty lines marked *Child* which are numbered by groups in
each section of dialogue preceding a song. These parts can be divided
among all children or assigned to one or several groups of children.
(See Production Notes on Cueing Children.)

Musicians

You will also need up to twelve children to play simple
instrumentation on "Play Our Praise." If you choose to open your
production with live music or need to extend the length of the
"Opening Music," you will need a pianist, organist, and any other
musicians who should sit to the right or left of the children. You
might also want to incorporate your Adult Choir in the Opening. *(See
Opening Options in Production Notes.)*

Solos

Only three of the twenty solos are assigned to a specific character.
The five solos in "Praise Medley" can be sung by any adult or child.

Younger Children

Ages 4-7 could enter with the Minister after "I'll Boast About Jesus"
and participate in the chorus of "Worthy of Worship," parts of "Praise
Medley," and "Levite Genes." An added line from the Minister like,
"Is it all right if the little ones join you?" would create the transition.

Opening Music
Holy, Holy, Holy Intro

Music by
JOHN B. DYKES
Arranged by Chris Marion

Hymn-like

("Holy, Holy, Holy Intro" denotes the end of the offertory. As the music ends, the Minister stands at the stage right pulpit and addresses the congregation. [See Opening Options in the Production Notes.])

MINISTER: Thank you. I certainly hope everyone appreciates our musicians as they serve God with their time and talents. *(optional applause)* With that in mind, our Children's Choir directors, Mr. Key and Mrs. Duffy, have asked me to announce that they will remain in the choir loft after service to distribute *(chuckling)* "Levite genes" to any children interested. Now, until we meet again, may the Lord bless you and keep you, may His face shine upon you, and may He grant you peace. Amen.

Play Our Praise Outro

Music by
KATHIE HILL
Arranged by Chris Marion

(As "Play Our Praise Outro" is played, the children enter excitedly from throughout the congregation to occupy the choir loft, as optional adult choir members yield the loft to them. The Minister exits stage right while Mr. Key and Mrs. Duffy come from the choir or congregation. Mr. Key takes his place behind the stage left music stand while Mrs. Duffy takes her place behind the stage right music stand.)

MRS. DUFFY: Well, it looks like every child here wants to be in the Children's Choir. That's great!

CHILD 1: The choir? I'm here for the jeans, Mrs. Duffy.

CHILD 2: Yeah … I like mine saggy and baggy!

CHILD 3: Make mine a western cut, Mr. Key.

MR. KEY: Oh, I'm afraid you misunderstood. We're not passing out Levite "j-e-a-n-s" jeans, but we want everyone to have Levite "g-e-n-e-s" genes.

ALL: Huh? What do they mean? "G-e-n-e-s?" I don't understand, *etc.*

CHILD 4: Mr. Key, I think *our* DNA is pretty well intact, *(proudly)* unless you're planning on cloning *me!*

MR. KEY: If only that were possible! But I think God broke the mold when He made you!

(Children laugh.)

MR. KEY: Besides, I'd want to be a copy of Jesus, becoming more like Him everyday.

ALL: *(agreeing)* Me, too! Yeah!, *etc.*

CHILD 5: So, Mrs. Duffy, what are you talking about when you say "Levite genes?"

MRS. DUFFY: We'll just use the phrase "Levite genes" to describe an inward desire to praise the Lord, something that's given by God when we're saved, and that we act on as we grow in Christ.

CHILD 6: So why are we just hearing about them now?

MRS. DUFFY: Because the pastor wants you children to lead worship next month. But Mr. Key and I realize you can't really do that without having a new song in your heart and Levite genes in your soul.

CHILD 7: But, what if I don't want to sing in the choir?

CHILD 8: Yeah. That's girls' stuff!

(Boys groan.)

MR. KEY: Ah, but most of the singers in the Old Testament were men.

MRS. DUFFY: Mr. Key's right. And worshiping God is not a chore, but a privilege for Christians. However, to lead worship wholeheartedly, it's helpful to have Levite genes. Does anyone know who the Levites were?

CHILD 9: Weren't they one of the twelve tribes of Israel?

MRS. DUFFY: Yes, one of Jacob's twelve sons was named Levi, so all of his descendants were called "Levites." And when Moses spent forty days and nights on Mount Sinai, what did the twelve tribes left behind do?

CHILD 10: They made a golden calf and worshiped it.

MRS. DUFFY: Yes. But when Moses came down and called for all who were still on the Lord's side, only the Levites came forward. That's why the Levites were special to God.

MR. KEY: I can just see old Moses now, looking over that multitude of people and saying, "Whoever is for the Lord, say so."

CHILD 11: *(loudly)* So!

(Children laugh.)

(Mr. Key and Mrs. Duffy remain standing at music stands and very subtly direct the children. They may do this on each song.)

Whoever Is for the Lord

Words and Music by
KATHIE HILL
Arranged by Chris Marion

*Circled measures indicate key points in the music notated in the **Dovetailor** teaching materials.*

Third time to Coda ⊕

for-ward and be heard, as you choose to be a child of

Third time to Coda ⊕

G#m   C#7(♭9)   F#m7   B13 B7

4/42 first time   (21)

God.
1. Here's your chance to ral - ly 'round the
2. Here's your chance to fol - low God with

E   B/D# C#m B   B/D# E   E/G#

King   of   kings.   Here's your chance to lift your voice and
all   your   heart.   Here's your chance for you to have a

A   B   E   B   B/D#   E   E/G#

sing,   sing,   sing.   Here's your chance to choose your side, your
brand   new   start.   Here's your chance to turn your back on

F#   F#/A#   B   A   E/G#

CHILD 1A: So, just what did the Levites do, Mr. Key?

MR. KEY: Their job was to plan the worship and take care of the temple. In fact, during King David's reign, there were four groups of Levites. The first were helpers to the priests—like our associate pastor(s).

CHILD 2A: What's the old saying? "We're number two and we try harder!"

(Children laugh in response.)

MR. KEY: You may be right. But there were also judges and scribes.

CHILD 3A: What's a scribe, Mrs. Duffy?

MRS. DUFFY: Someone who writes everything down.

CHILD 4A: I couldn't do that—nobody could read my handwriting!

(Children respond in agreement.)

MR. KEY: And the third group were doormen, or doorkeepers. These Levites lived in the temple and protected the doors, opening them only for those allowed to enter.

CHILD 5A: Sounds like a "grunt job."

MRS. DUFFY: Oh, but doorkeeping must have been pretty important to God. As a child, I learned a verse that says, "I would rather be a doorkeeper in the house of my God, than dwell in the tents of the wicked."* What do you think that means?

CHILD 6A: That it's better to be a servant of God than be a "big dog" with sinners?

MRS. DUFFY: Yes. But it takes strength and courage to stand for God when you're tempted.

CHILD 7A: What do you mean?

MR. KEY: Well, just imagine this scenario. You children, come help me out.

*Psalm 84:10

(Children help the Ruler into his costume, stage left, and Mrs. Duffy helps the Boy into his costume, stage right. They take their places opposite each other, center stage or at the center stage railing.)

CHILD 8A: What are they doing with those costumes?

(Music begins.)

CHILD 9A: They're dressing up like characters.

CHILD 10A: Look! They're going to act out the song!

A Doorman for the Lord

Words and Music by
KATHIE HILL
Arranged by Chris Marion

(Ruler and Boy remove their costumes offstage and take their original positions.)

ALL:	That was cool! Good job, guys, *etc.*

CHILD 1B: Mrs. Duffy, you said the Levites took care of the temple. But I thought there wasn't a real temple until King Solomon's day.

MRS. DUFFY: You're correct. Before the temple was built in Jerusalem, God's people worshiped in the wilderness in a tabernacle, or tent.

CHILD 2B: Cool. I'd like that!

ALL: Uh, huh. Me, too, *etc.*

MRS. DUFFY: And it was the Levites' responsibility to carry the furniture and set up the tent every time they moved.

CHILD 2B: On second thought, maybe I wouldn't!

(Children laugh.)

CHILD 3B: Don't forget the ark, Mrs. Duffy.

CHILD 4B: Duh! The ark was in Noah's time … long before Moses.

CHILD 3B: I mean the ark of the covenant. It was like a holy wooden crate where the ten commandments were kept.

MRS. DUFFY: Yes, the Levites were responsible for the ark of the covenant and all the holy objects. Right, Mr. Key?

MR. KEY: That's because the Levites were representatives of God's *holiness.* So how can *we* worship God unless *we* understand His holiness?

CHILD 5B: I think we sang a hymn about God's holiness in service today.

MRS. DUFFY: I think you're right.

Holy, Holy, Holy

Words by
REGINALD HEBER

Music by
JOHN B. DYKES
Arranged by Chris Marion and Kathie Hill

1. Ho - ly, ho - ly,
2. Ho - ly, ho - ly,

God in three Per - sons, bless - ed Trin - i -
Who wert, and art, and ev - er - more shalt

ty!
be.

3. Ho - ly, ho - ly, ho - ly! tho' the dark - ness

CHILD 1C:	That's my Mom's favorite hymn, Mr. Key.
MR. KEY:	Mine, too, because it comes from the book of The Revelation where, in heaven, we join with the angels to worship Christ.
CHILD 2C:	You mean sing with the seraphim and cherubim?
MR. KEY:	Yes. The hymn mentions those angels. But, what does that hymn tell us about God?
CHILD 3C:	That God is holy.
CHILD 4C:	That He is merciful and mighty.
CHILD 5C:	That He is the Blessed Trinity.
MR. KEY:	That means the Father, Son, and Holy Spirit. Anything else?
CHILD 6C:	That God is adored and the angels fall before Him.
CHILD 7C:	And that even the earth, sky, and sea will praise His name.
MRS. DUFFY:	So, if trees and rocks and oceans and mountains will eventually praise God, shouldn't we praise Him now?
CHILD 8C:	Sure, Mrs. Duffy. But if we're gonna praise God in heaven, we'd better learn some songs here on earth.
CHILD 9C:	Yeah, but where do we begin?
CHILD 10C:	I can sing a solo … so low you can't hear me!
(Children laugh.)	
MRS. DUFFY:	That's exactly why we got you together to rehearse today … because the fourth group of Levites were the musicians.
MR. KEY:	Great musicians who sang in worship, sang before battles, at funerals, and for dedications of the temple. When there was a need for praise, the Levites had a song.
CHILD 11C:	Where did these songs come from?
MRS. DUFFY:	Most of them were from the writings of David. In addition to being a king and a warrior, David wrote song after song …
CHILD 12C:	… after *psalm*.
MRS. DUFFY:	Yes. The book of Psalms is the Bible's hymnbook. And of the one hundred fifty psalms, seventy-three were written by David. Would you like to learn what was probably the first of David's psalms?
ALL:	Sure. Yeah, let's hear it. Can we?, *etc.*
MRS. DUFFY:	The original tune has been long forgotten, but, like all the Bible, the words will remain forever.

Give Thanks to the Lord
(David's Psalm)

Words based on
1 Chronicles 16:8-12

Music by
KATHIE HILL
Arranged by Chris Marion

CHILD 1D: So all the last group of Levites did was sing?

MR. KEY: Sing and *play.*

CHILD 2D: Play! That sounds like my kind of job!

ALL: (*responding*) Yeah. Mine, too, *etc.*

MR. KEY: No … play *instruments.* These Levites were accomplished vocalists and instrumentalists. Why, King David alone had 4,000 singers as temple musicians.

MRS. DUFFY: David also had drummers, trumpeters, flautists, and harpists, along with cymbal and psaltery players.

(*Mrs. Duffy brings out a box of instruments from stage left and begins placing them on the choir railing or table. [See Props List for specific instruments or substitutions.]*)

CHILD 3D: "Salty" players?

MR. KEY: No, *psaltery* players. The psaltery was a kind of harp that's no longer played today. But, some of the Levite instruments are like those Mrs. Duffy is bringing out now.

ALL: (*responding*) I recognize a lot of them. Hey, I've seen *that* before, *etc.*

MRS. DUFFY: These instruments represent some of the many ways to praise the Lord. If you can play one of these instruments, why not come up and help us worship?

(*Children respond enthusiastically and instrumentalists move to their instruments.*)

CHILD 4D: But, I've never played in church before.

MRS. DUFFY: Well, if God gave you the talent to play, shouldn't you use it for Him?

CHILD 4D: I guess you're right.

MRS. DUFFY: I know I am!

Play Our Praise

Words and Music by
KATHIE HILL
Arranged by Chris Marion

*If using "live" music, those playing the instrument listed may play the notes in brackets. Nonpitched instruments (cymbals, drums, tambourine, etc.) should play the rhythm indicated in brackets. Bb Trumpet and Bb Clarinet must play the notes a whole step higher than indicated. Wherever instruments are used, the pianist may ignore the bracketed notes (except where piano is the specified instrument). If only piano is used, all bracketed notes should be played. All instruments play together starting on page 36.

34

43

19/57 **first time**

You, play our praise un - to the Lord

FLUTE/VIOLIN

(play)

B♭ TRUMPET/B♭ CLARINET

(play)

BELLS

CYMBALS

TRIANGLE

DRUMS

STICKS

TAMBOURINE

WOODBLOCK

| F#m | B9 | Em | Em/A | 1 D | D/F# |

(Children laugh and commend themselves as Mrs. Starr enters down the center aisle and takes her place center stage.)

MRS. STARR: Pardon me, but how long will it be before the children get their Levite jeans? I don't care what my little Lucy wears, as long as I can get her home in time to practice for her Swishy Wishy Car Wash commercial.

LUCY: *(embarrassed)* But, Mother ...

MRS. DUFFY: Mrs. Starr, we're sorry to keep you waiting. We're just going over some songs we'll be singing in worship.

MRS. STARR: Did you say "sing?" Well, I hope you've given Lucy a solo. You've probably heard her on the Choco Chums jingle. Sing it for them, Lucy!

LUCY: Mom, please!

MRS. STARR: *(ignoring her)* Lucy's had three years of voice lessons, plus six years of ballet, tap, and jazz. So, I'm sure you have a very special part for her.

MR. KEY: All the children have special parts, Mrs. Starr, because all of them are singing to praise the Lord. Why don't you sit here on the platform until we finish? I promise, it won't be long.

MRS. STARR: All right. I'll just sit here and fill out this Little Miss* Pageant entry form that's due tomorrow.

(Mrs. Starr moves to a stage right chair, sits in the chair, and pulls out paper and pencil from her purse to begin writing.)

*Add the name of your city.

MR. KEY: Let's see. Where were we?

CHILD 1E: We just *played* our praise to the Lord!

MR. KEY: Oh, yes. David mentions many instruments in his psalms.

CHILD 2E: So, which is the best psalm, Mrs. Duffy?

MRS. DUFFY: Well, all the psalms are special in their own way, because they express so many of the same emotions we feel. But one psalm comes to mind that the Levites sang at the completion of the temple.

CHILD 3E: Solomon's temple?

MRS. DUFFY: *(picking up a Bible)* Yes. Solomon built the temple his father, David, had planned. *(turning to the correct page)* Here, read how the Bible describes the scene and see if you don't think David would have been pleased with how his song was used. *(She hands the Bible to child)*

CHILD 4E: *(reading from the Bible)* All the Levites who were musicians … stood on the east side of the altar, dressed in fine linen and playing cymbals, harps, and lyres. They were accompanied by one hundred twenty priests sounding trumpets. The trumpeters and singers joined in unison, as with one voice, to give praise and thanks to the Lord.

(Sound effect of wind blowing*)

CHILD 4E: *(over the wind sounds)* Then the temple of the Lord was filled with a cloud, and the priests could not perform their service because of the cloud, for the glory of the Lord filled the temple of God.**

*The sound effect of wind blowing appears on the Accompaniment CD at

**2 Chronicles 5:12-14

He Is Good

Words and Music by
KATHIE HILL
Arranged by Chris Marion

MRS. STARR: My, that was beautiful! The only improvement would be to have my Lucy read one of the scriptures. She has such a lovely speaking voice—haven't you heard her on the commercial for the Chicken Lickin' House?

MRS. DUFFY: Yes, I have, Mrs. Starr. But we want the children to learn that worship doesn't draw attention to one individual, but that together, we draw attention to God.

MRS. STARR: Well, I suppose you're right. This *is* church. But you must admit, Lucy is multi-talented.

MR. KEY: As are all of our children. That's why, just as there were different groups of Levites, there are many ways these children can lead others to worship.

CHILD 1F: You mean my drawings could help people to worship?

MR. KEY: Of course, especially if they depict God's goodness or the beauty of His creation.

CHILD 2F: I'm learning to sew!

MRS. DUFFY: Then you could make robes for the choir.

CHILD 3F: My dad is teaching me to run the sound board.

MR. KEY: That's very necessary for our worship. If we're going to praise the Lord, we certainly want everyone to hear us!

ALL: (*approvingly*) Yeah, *etc.*

MRS. STARR: (*insistently*) Especially my little Lucy!

LUCY: Mother, I know you think I'm wonderful, but all these children deserve to be bragged on, too.

MRS. DUFFY: Lucy's right. But, instead of bragging on anyone, let's do what the Bible says and "boast in the Lord."

LUCY: Isn't that what praise really is—boasting about Jesus?

MRS. STARR: (*totally confused*) But, darling, I don't understand.

LUCY: Just listen.

(*Lucy should sing stage right between her mother and Mrs. Duffy or from behind the railing, to keep from drawing the attention she is trying to redirect to the Lord.*)

I'll Boast About Jesus

Words and Music by
KATHIE HILL
Arranged by Chris Marion

1. Did you ev-er meet a man who __ al-ways had his hand a-pat-tin' him-self on the back?

(2.) Bi-ble makes it clear that a bod-y ought to steer a-way from brag-gin' on him-self.

54
CHOIR
(opt. div.)
I'll boast a - bout Je - sus, I'll boast of
Gb N.C.
Cb6
Cb
Cb
57
know-in' the Lord.
Of His love and His grace, I'm
Gb
Gb
Abm
Gb/Bb
60
gon - na shout.
These are the things I'll boast a - bout. A-bout
Cb
C°7
Gb/Db
Db7(add 13)
Gb
63
Je - sus, I'll boast of know-in' the Lord.
Cb6
Cb
Cb
Gb

(Children respond enthusiastically to the song. Minister enters from stage left and stands in front of the chair.)

MINISTER: Well, this sounds like the place to be!

CHILD 1G: Oh, pastor, thanks for asking us to sing next month.

ALL: Yeah, we can't wait. Thanks a lot, pastor, *etc.*

CHILD 1G: We've been learning some great songs *and* learning all about the Levites.

CHILD 2G: They *were* the first worship leaders, you know.

MINISTER: In the Old Testament. But the wonderful news of the New Testament is that anyone can worship if they have Jesus in their heart.

MRS. DUFFY: The Levites had to be born into the tribe of Levi to praise the Lord, but we just need to be "born again."

MR. KEY: Yes, sir. When you become a Christian, the Bible says you have a new song to sing.

MINISTER: Mr. Key is right. But, did you know the early Christians weren't allowed to worship in the temple like the Levites? They had to worship in their homes or in hiding places.

CHILD 3G: You mean they worshiped in secret?

MRS. DUFFY: Yes. But their persecution, or unfair treatment, only made them trust Jesus more. The Bible says they praised God with "psalms and hymns and spiritual songs," making music in their hearts to the Lord.

MR. KEY: The early Christians sang old songs of what God had done in the past and new songs about the life, death, and resurrection of His Son, Jesus.

CHILD 4G: Sounds like they had Levite genes!

(Children respond in agreement.)

MINISTER: Yes. In spite of great opposition, they chose to worship God, because God is *worthy* of our praise.

(Minister sits in stage left chair and, along with Mrs. Starr, watches children sing.)

Worthy of Worship

Words by
TERRY W. YORK

Music by
MARK BLANKENSHIP
Arranged by Chris Marion

CHILD 1H:	So, pastor*, do you think we've got Levite genes yet?
ALL:	(responding) Yeah, What do you think?, etc.
MINISTER:	(standing) Well, praise is an overflow of the heart. So, if you've trusted Jesus and love Him with all your heart, then you can't help but choose to praise Him. And I guess that's what I'd call having Levite genes.

(Children respond enthusiastically.)

MRS. STARR:	(standing apologetically) Oh, Mrs. Duffy. I'm afraid I've been all wrong about what you're doing with these children. My heart has only been thinking of how wonderful *my* child is, not how wonderful the Lord is. How can I possibly make it up to you?
MRS. DUFFY:	Well, Mrs. Starr, it's obvious that you're very organized, getting Lucy to all her auditions and lessons and such. Why don't you become our choir secretary? You could keep the attendance records and remind the children of when we sing.
MRS. STARR:	(excited) And that could be *my* way of worshiping, right?
MR. KEY:	Worship always expresses itself in service. And that would certainly be a great service to us.
CHILD 2H:	So, pastor*, what would you like us to sing next month?
ALL:	(responding) What would you like? Which song? Yes, what should we sing? *etc.*
MINISTER:	Well, I love the psalms and hymns you've been learning, but I'd like to teach the congregation some new praise choruses. Simple songs which teach us the character of God and help us worship Him for who He is.
CHILD 3H:	They'd *better* be simple, cause there's a lot of people in the congregation who never even open their mouths!
MINISTER:	Yes. And that's why we need to be like the Levites … to make our praise so enthusiastic, they can't help but join us. Here, let Mrs. Duffy show you.**

(Minister and Mrs. Starr remain standing and join in on choir parts.
**Anyone can sing the first solo. If it is the Minister, change line to "Here, let
me show you." A similar change would be needed to introduce Mr. Key or
any of the children.)

*Insert person's name.

Praise Medley

With strength! (♩ = 86)

Arranged by Chris Marion and Kathie Hill

First time - MRS. DUFFY SOLO
Second time - CHOIR

*What a won-der-ful Lord to be wor-shiped and _ a-dored. Your Word is blessed a-mong _ the na- tions. I will praise Your _ name, _ to the

SOLO: Have you heard this one?

SOLO: This chorus is pretty!

*"Prince of Peace," Words and music by KATHIE HILL. © Copyright 1995 Van Ness Press, Inc. (ASCAP). Distributed by GENEVOX (a div. of GMG), Nashville, TN 37234.

First time - SOLO
Second time - CHOIR

Both times - CHOIR

breath I take, God I will

Db   Bbm7   Eb

First time - SOLO
Second time - CHOIR

Both times - CHOIR

praise You. With ev-'ry word I speak, new hope I

Db/Ab   Ab   Db   Bbm7   Eb

First time - SOLO
Second time - SOLO

sing. When I lie down at night, or when I

Ab   Db/Ab   Ab   Fm7   Bbm7   Fm/Ab   Eb/G

Both times - CHOIR [1

greet the morn-ing light, Love of my heart, prais-es to You, glad-ly I

Ab   Eb/G   Fm7   Fm7/Eb   [1 Db   Bbm7   Eb

MINISTER: Now, let me really hear you lift your praise!

(Minister, Mrs. Starr, Mrs. Duffy, and Mr. Key applaud.)

MRS. STARR: *(proudly)* That was wonderful! *(quickly explaining)* But, of course, my applause is for the Lord.

MINISTER: Yes, I know. But we're applauding the children's efforts, too.

MRS. DUFFY: Children, now you know a little of the time and hard work it takes to prepare for worship.

MR. KEY: That's what the Bible means when it talks about the "sacrifice of praise." It will take many more rehearsals before we're ready to lead worship … and a lot of prayer to ensure that our hearts are right before the Lord.

CHILD 1I: Time, talent, and a holy heart. That's what the Levites gave the Lord.

MINISTER: Yes, and if you give those things to Him, I'd say your Levite genes are a perfect fit!

(Children laugh and respond enthusiastically.)

Levite Genes

Words and Music by
KATHIE HILL
Arranged by Chris Marion

See Closing Options in Production Notes.

Exit Music
(Levite Genes Reprise)

Words and Music by
KATHIE HILL
Arranged by Chris Marion

Production Notes

Opening Options

Opening Intro (Holy, Holy, Holy Intro)

• You may use the Accompaniment CD or Cassette from the beginning and play an entire stanza of "Holy, Holy, Holy," during which children enter and take places in the congregation.

• You may already have children in congregation and fade up the Accompaniment CD or Cassette at any point in the music.

• You may use your own musicians to play the last stanza, with optional choir members singing in the loft.

• You may use your own musicians to play the hymn while you actually take an offering and lead into the musical with no introduction.

Opening Outro (Play Our Praise Outro)

If one chorus of "Play Our Praise" is not enough to get your children from the congregation into the choir loft, have musicians play enough repeats of the chorus until all children are settled, then fade out.

Closing Options

• Because of the nature and message of this musical, the "Exit Music" is provided not for bows, but for the audience's continued applause or to allow the children to rejoin their families in the congregation.

• If an invitation is to be given, children can repeat "He Is Good" as an invitation song, then exit to the "Exit Music" after they have been corporately recognized.

• To further involve the congregation, the Minister might want to repeat "Praise Medley" to end the service, then have children exit to the "Exit Music."

• If children wish to sing along with the "Exit Music," the vocals are printed and may be heard on the Split-Track of the CD or Accompaniment Cassette.

Choir

Arranging Children

Since the children do not line up somewhere and enter to their particular row, have them sit with their families or toward the front of the congregation. Place a piece of masking tape with their name written on it so they can find their place when they enter the loft or stage. Organize your choir to look disorganized!

Cueing Children

If the child speaking parts are divided throughout the choir, use a washable marker to write the part(s) number on one or both hands, i.e. 3 or 3f, etc. Try to give children with multiple lines the same number, i.e. 4, 4b, 4d, 4g, etc. Have a cue card made for every dialogue number and instruct someone to hold up the cue cards just before the children should move to the microphone. If using a small group of children to perform all Child lines, assign each a number 1-10 (1-12 or 1-15) so they will always speak in the same sequence.

Microphones

The stage diagram suggests four mics for the child speakers and soloists. To accommodate different heights of the children, you may lay these mics on the railing or allow children to take them out of the stand, pass them to the speaker behind them, or place them back on the railing or stand. These mics are labeled 1-4 and speakers should use the mic that matches or corresponds to his or her part number. Speakers 1-4 use mics 1-4, speakers 5-9 start again with mic 1-4, and 10-14 begin again with mic 1-4.

Mr. Key and Mrs. Duffy can have mic stands placed slightly to their left and right, so that when they speak they are turned 3/4 or diagonally on the stage, speaking to both the children and the "imaginary" audience.

Because of their movement, Mrs. Starr and the Minister should be on lavaliere mics. If the Minister sings in "Praise Medley," he may borrow Mr. Key's microphone for any solo.

Costumes

Children may wear their Sunday morning or Sunday evening clothes. (Sunday evening clothes could include blue jeans and nice tops, but not matching T-shirts as this choir is just being organized.) Mrs. Duffy and Mr. Key are in choir robes or Sunday clothes. Mrs. Starr wears an overly fancy Sunday dress and hat. The Minister may wear a robe or suit at the beginnning, and remove his suit coat or robe for his ending entrance.

The Ruler can quickly slip into a king's robe and turban and the Boy into a shabby child's tunic and headband. Other children can help with these quick costume add-ons.

Options for solos in "A Doorman for the Lord:"

• Mr. Key can don a king's costume and sing the Ruler's solo.

• A child may use a chair or box to elevate himself and don a floor length king's robe to create the illusion of an adult. That child may sing the Ruler's solo in his own octave, or lip-sync to an offstage adult soloist.

• A boy (or girl dressed as a boy) can sing the Boy's solo. Both the Ruler and the Boy should act out the lyrics.

(These costumes and options are demonstrated on the Instructional/ Movement Video.)

Choreography, Movement, and Visuals

Since this musical emphasizes corporate praise and worship rather than elevating one child or another, the use of choreography should be handled discreetly. The *Dovetailor* gives instructions on making banners for "Worthy of Worship" and includes reproducible lyric sheets for all the choruses in "Praise Medley," to be shown on an overhead projector or Image Max. Another use of slides or video would be to show images of the instrumentalists in "Play Our Praise" and other musicians in your church or community. Other choreography suggestions for the remaining songs are demonstrated on the Instructional/Movemement Video.

Set and Staging

The setting for *Levite Genes* is the pulpit and choir loft of a church or worship area. If performing in another room, create a colorful background by making stained glass windows out of colored tissue paper or transparencies and mount banners behind the children. Potted plants and a floral arrangement can decorate the platform. The Minister's pulpit should be stage right so as not to block the view of the children. (Set suggestions are demonstrated on the Instructional/Movement Video.)

There should be a platform chair on both stage right and stage left which will eventually be occupied by Mrs. Starr and the Minister. Mr. Key stands at stage left and Mrs. Duffy at stage right, subtly directing the children as they sing, but never blocking or upstaging them.

All staging directions are included within the script, with the placement of speakers indicated on the *Staging Diagram.*

If there is a choir railing in your performance area, set solo microphones between the railing and the first row of children. This will make it easier for the speaker and soloists to get to the microphones and will add to the sense of corporate worship. If there are chairs in your choir loft, remove them or don't allow children to sit between songs, as it will distract from the dialogue.

Props

- small pulpit or lectern with optional drape
- potted plants/floral arrangement in front of pulpit
- platform chairs on right and left of the platform
- music stands on stage right and left for Mr. Key and Mrs. Duffy
- box filled with a variety of instruments such as trumpet, flute, recorder, cymbals, woodblock and mallet, sticks, violin, autoharp, clarinet, triangle, bongo drums, piano or electric keyboard, tambourine for "Play Our Praise"
- Bible for Mrs. Duffy
- smoke machine for scripture reading and "He Is Good" *(opt.)*
- paper entry form and pencil for Mrs. Starr's purse
- four praise banners for "Worthy of Worship" (Father, Creator, Savior, Sustainer*) *(opt.)*
- overhead projector, screen, and blank transparencies for reproducible "Praise Medley" lyrics and musician slides in "Play Our Praise."

These and optional flying banners for "Give Thanks to the Lord" are shown on the Instructional / Movement Video.

Stage Diagram

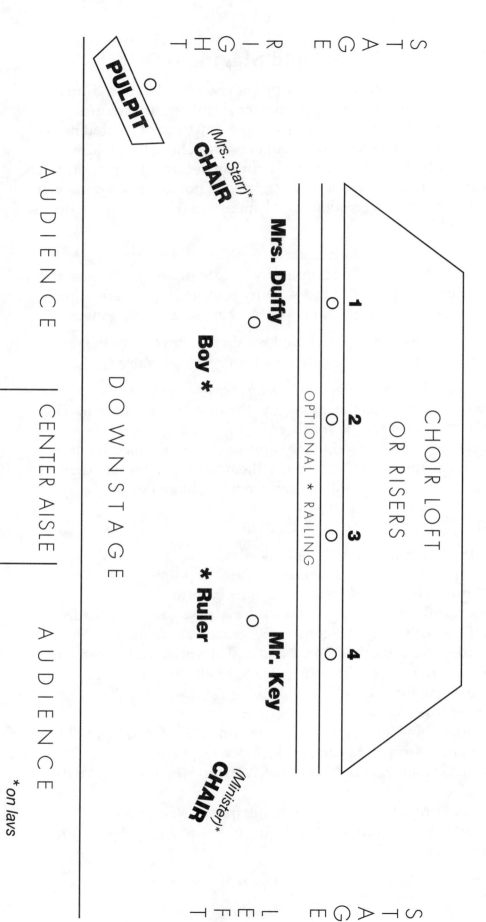

Levite Genes

A PRAISE AND WORSHIP MUSICAL FOR CHILDREN BY

Kathie Hill